My love for you goes everywhere,
and anywhere you go.
It follows you both day and night,
through rain and sun and snow.

You might not always see my love,
but it goes everywhere.

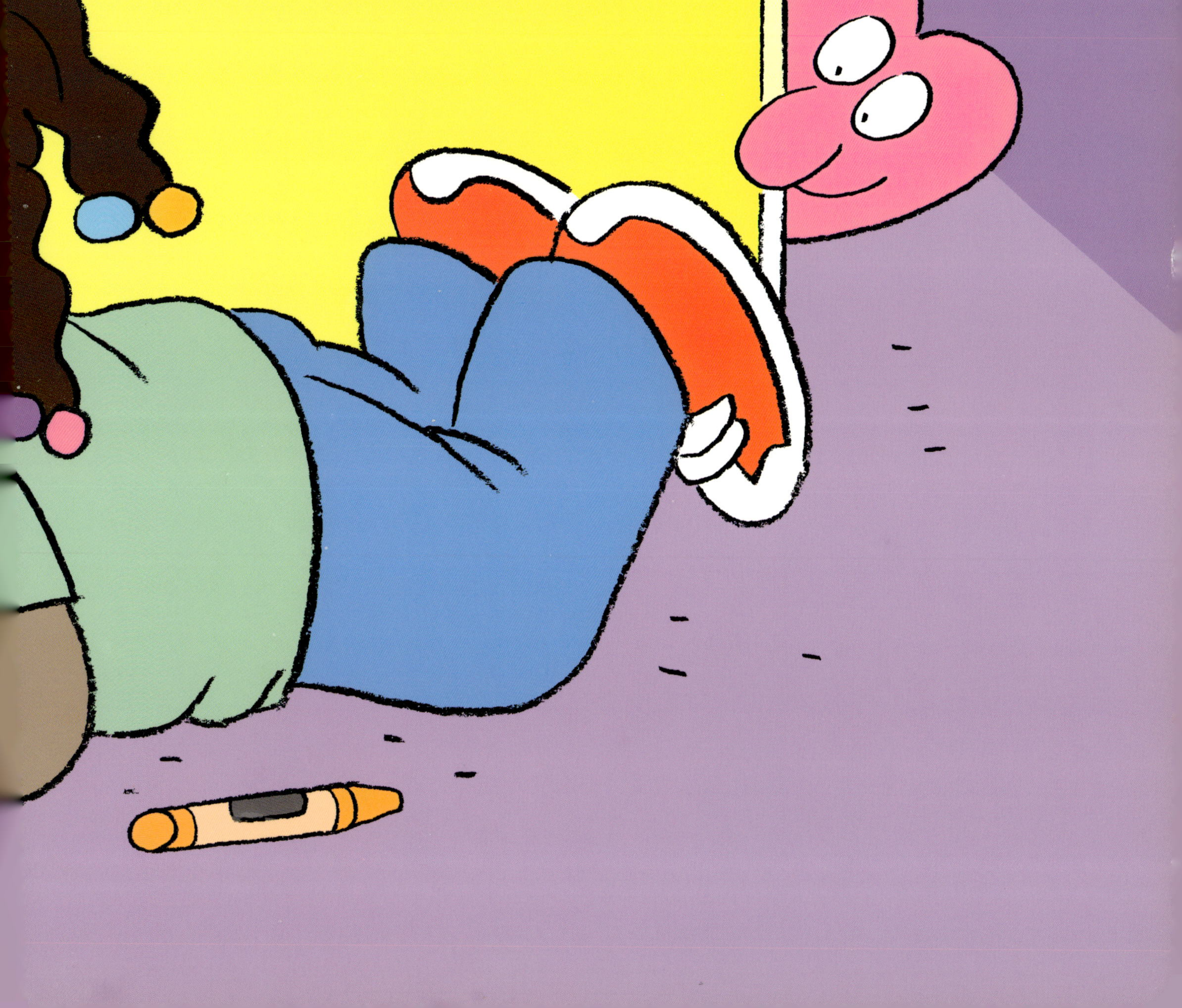

Even if you go out walking
in your underwear!

You might be inside a pig pen
or on a dinosaur.
My love will be there next to you.
(Don't ride those anymore.)

Underneath a turtle
could be where it might hide.

Or among some pink flamingos
(providing you're outside).

And while you sleep in bed at night
my love is waiting there.

And doesn't care that when you snore,
you're louder than a bear!

And no matter where you travel.
No matter what you say.